HEARTSTRINGS OF LOVE

SAYAN BANIK

Made with ♥ on the Notion Press Platform
www.notionpress.com

For all the lovers and dreamers out there, this book is for you.

Contents

Acknowledgements

I would like to express my heartfelt gratitude to everyone who has been a part of the creation of this book, "Heartstrings of Love," particularly those who have supported me throughout my writing journey.

Firstly, I would like to extend my sincere thanks to my family and friends, who have always been a source of encouragement, motivation, and support. They have been my constant companions, listening to my ideas, providing constructive feedback, and giving me the strength to keep going.

I would also like to acknowledge the editors and proofreaders who have worked tirelessly to ensure that this book is polished and error-free. Their insightful comments and suggestions have greatly enhanced the quality of the book.

I would like to extend my appreciation to the cover artist, whose stunning artwork perfectly captures the essence of the book. Their creativity has helped bring my vision to life.

Last but not least, I would like to thank my readers for their love and support. Writing is a labor of love, and it is the readers who make it all worthwhile. I hope that this book touches your heart and brings a smile to your face.

Thank you all for your support and encouragement.

Sincerely,

Sayan Banik

I

Ravi and Leela

Once upon a time, in a small village in India, there lived a young couple named Ravi and Leela. They had grown up together and had been in love since childhood. Ravi was a handsome and hardworking man, while Leela was a beautiful and kind-hearted woman. They had always dreamed of getting married and starting a family together.

However, their happiness was short-lived. One day, a group of bandits attacked their village, killing many innocent people and burning their homes to the ground. Ravi and Leela were lucky to escape, but they were separated in the chaos.

Ravi searched desperately for Leela for days, but he could not find her. He feared the worst and mourned her loss. However, after several weeks, he received word that Leela had been found, but she was not alone. She had been taken captive by one of the bandits, a cruel and heartless man named Vikram.

Ravi was devastated to hear this news, but he was determined to save Leela. He gathered a group of brave men and set out to rescue her from Vikram's clutches. After a long and difficult journey, they finally found Vikram's hideout and launched a surprise attack.

During the chaos of the battle, Ravi found Leela and they were finally reunited. They shared a tearful embrace, relieved to be back in each other's arms once again. However, their joy was short-lived, as Vikram emerged from the shadows with a dagger in his hand.

Ravi and Vikram engaged in a fierce battle, but Ravi was no match for the skilled bandit. In a tragic turn of events, Ravi was fatally wounded and fell to the ground. Leela rushed to his side, cradling him in her arms as he took his last breath.

Tears streamed down Leela's face as she mourned the loss of her beloved Ravi. She could not imagine a life without him, and her heart was shattered into a million pieces. As she wept, Vikram approached her with a wicked grin on his face.

Leela knew that she could not let Vikram take her as his captive again. In a moment of desperation, she pulled out a small dagger that she had hidden in her clothes and plunged it into her own heart. As she fell to the ground, she whispered Ravi's name one last time before taking her final breath.

The villagers who had accompanied Ravi on his mission were devastated to see the tragic end of such a beautiful love story. They buried Ravi and Leela together in a peaceful spot near the village. For years to come, people would tell the tale of Ravi and Leela, the star-crossed lovers who had lost everything but their love for each other.

Their love story was a reminder that even in the darkest of times, love can still conquer all. Though their time together was brief, their love was eternal and will be remembered forever.

II

Love Conquers All

Once upon a time, in a small village nestled in the hills of India, there lived a young woman named Priya. She was the daughter of a farmer and had grown up with a deep love for nature and a strong sense of responsibility towards her family.

One day, while walking through the fields, Priya met a handsome young man named Rahul. Rahul was a city boy who had come to the village to spend some time with his grandparents. He was immediately smitten with Priya's beauty and grace, and she was taken by his confident demeanor and charming smile.

As the days passed, Rahul and Priya found themselves spending more and more time together. They would walk through the fields, sit by the river, and talk for hours on end. It wasn't long before they realized that they had fallen in love.

However, there was a problem. Priya's father had already arranged for her to marry a wealthy landowner from a neighboring village. Priya was torn between her love for Rahul and her duty to her family.

Rahul, who had never been one to give up easily, decided to fight for his love. He approached Priya's father and asked for his blessing to marry Priya. At first, Priya's father was hesitant, but Rahul's sincerity and devotion won him over. He agreed to let Rahul marry Priya on one condition - that he prove himself worthy of her love.

Rahul accepted the challenge and set out to win the heart of his beloved. He worked hard in the fields, helped Priya's family with their chores, and showed them that he was willing to do whatever it took to be with Priya.

As the days passed, Rahul's love for Priya grew stronger. He knew that he couldn't live without her, and he was determined to prove it to her family. One day, he approached Priya's father and asked for one more chance to prove himself.

Priya's father agreed, and Rahul decided to take matters into his own hands. He organized a grand feast for the entire village and invited Priya's family as his special guests. He spent days preparing the food, decorating the village, and making sure that everything was perfect.

On the day of the feast, the village was alive with music, dancing, and laughter. Everyone was enjoying themselves, and Priya's family was impressed by Rahul's efforts. As the night wore on, Rahul took Priya aside and asked her to marry him. Priya, who had already fallen deeply in love with Rahul, said yes without hesitation.

Priya's father, who had been watching from afar, realized that Rahul was indeed worthy of his daughter's love. He approached Rahul and gave him his blessing, and the couple was married in a grand ceremony that was attended by the entire village.

Rahul and Priya lived happily ever after, and their love became a legend in the village. They worked hard, raised a family, and never forgot the lessons they learned about love, devotion, and determination. They were a shining example of what true love could be, and their story continued to inspire generations to come.

III

Lotus Blossoms

Once upon a time, in a small village in India, there lived a young man named Ravi. Ravi was a kind and gentle soul who spent his days working hard in the fields and helping his neighbors. Despite his many good qualities, Ravi was a lonely man, for he had never found love.

One day, while Ravi was walking through the fields, he spotted a beautiful young woman named Maya. Maya was the daughter of the village's chief and was known throughout the village for her beauty and kindness. Ravi was immediately smitten by her and began to find reasons to be near her. Over time, Ravi and Maya became friends, and Ravi fell deeply in love with her.

As time went by, Ravi and Maya's friendship grew stronger, and Ravi knew that he had to tell her how he felt. He gathered his courage and confessed his love to her. To his delight, Maya reciprocated his feelings, and they became a couple.

Ravi and Maya spent many happy days together, walking through the fields, talking for hours, and enjoying each other's company. They were so in love that they often talked about getting married and starting a family.

However, their happiness was not to last. One day, while Ravi was working in the fields, a group of bandits attacked the village. Maya, who had been in her house at the time, was taken captive by the bandits and carried away.

Ravi was devastated when he learned of Maya's capture. He immediately set out to rescue her, determined to do whatever it took to bring her back to safety. He traveled for days, finally reaching the bandit's hideout deep in the mountains.

There, Ravi fought bravely against the bandits, determined to save Maya. However, he was outnumbered and outmatched, and he was eventually captured and imprisoned with Maya.

Ravi and Maya were kept prisoner in a small, dark cell. Despite their dire circumstances, they remained devoted to each other, finding comfort in their love for one another. They talked for hours, imagining their life together if they were to escape and be reunited.

However, their hopes were dashed when the bandits announced that they were going to kill them both. Ravi and Maya held each other tightly, refusing to be separated even in death.

As the bandits prepared to execute them, Maya whispered to Ravi that she loved him and always would. Ravi responded by promising to love her forever, even beyond death.

And with those words, the bandits carried out their cruel act, ending the lives of Ravi and Maya. As they lay side by side, their hands still clasped tightly, a single lotus flower bloomed in the darkness of their cell.

The villagers, hearing of Ravi and Maya's tragic end, were heartbroken. They held a funeral for the couple, burying them side by side in a field of lotus flowers. And it was said that from that day forward, every year, on the anniversary of their death, a single lotus flower would bloom on their graves, a reminder of their love and devotion.

IV

True Love in the Kingdom

Once upon a time, in the land of India, there lived a beautiful princess named Rani. She was the daughter of the king of the land, and was known throughout the kingdom for her grace, intelligence, and kind heart. Her beauty was such that poets would write songs about her, and travelers would come from far and wide just to catch a glimpse of her.

One day, a handsome prince named Raj came to the kingdom. He was from a neighboring land, and had come to seek the hand of Princess Rani in marriage. The king was delighted at the prospect of such a match, and welcomed the prince with open arms.

Raj was struck by the beauty of Princess Rani as soon as he saw her. He was awestruck by her poise and elegance, and was convinced that she was the woman he had been searching for his entire life. Princess Rani, too, was charmed by the prince's good looks and easy charm, and the two quickly fell in love.

The days that followed were filled with laughter and joy. Raj would take Princess Rani on long walks through the palace gardens, where they would sit and watch the stars come out at night. They would talk for hours, sharing stories about their pasts, their dreams, and their hopes for the future.

As the weeks turned into months, Raj and Princess Rani grew closer and closer. They knew that they were meant to be together, and they began to make plans for their future. Raj knew that he wanted to spend the rest of his life with Princess Rani, and he began to make preparations for their wedding.

Finally, the day of the wedding arrived. The palace was decorated with flowers and candles, and guests from all over the kingdom had come to witness the union of two souls. Princess Rani looked resplendent in her bridal attire, with her hair adorned with flowers and her eyes shining with joy.

As the wedding ceremony began, Raj and Princess Rani exchanged vows of love and commitment. They promised to stand by each other through thick and thin, through joy and sorrow, for all the days of their lives. And as they sealed their promises with a kiss, the guests erupted into cheers and applause.

The rest of the evening was filled with music, dance, and feasting. Raj and Princess Rani danced together, lost in the beauty of the moment. They knew that they had found true love, and they were grateful for every moment that they spent together.

As the night wore on, the guests began to depart one by one. Raj and Princess Rani retreated to their chambers, tired but happy. They snuggled under the covers, their hearts beating as one. They knew that their love was strong enough to conquer anything that life might throw at them.

And so, Raj and Princess Rani lived happily ever after. They had many children, and their love grew stronger with each passing day. They remained devoted to each other until the end of their days, and their love story became the stuff of legend in the land of India.

In conclusion, love stories like these are what make life worth living. It is the promise of eternal love that keeps us going, even when the road ahead is rocky and uncertain. May we all find a love as strong and enduring as that of Raj and Princess Rani.

V

The Blossoming of Love

Asha had always been a dreamer. She was the daughter of a wealthy merchant and lived a comfortable life in the bustling city of Mumbai. But despite her privileged upbringing, Asha longed for something more. She yearned for the kind of love that she had only ever read about in books.

One day, while on a shopping excursion with her mother, Asha met a young man named Rohit. He was tall and handsome with jet black hair and piercing brown eyes. Asha felt an instant attraction to him, and as luck would have it, Rohit felt the same way.

Over the next few weeks, Asha and Rohit began to see each other regularly. They would meet at cafes and restaurants, taking long walks through the city streets, talking for hours about their hopes and dreams. Asha felt as though she had finally found the love she had been searching for.

However, there was a problem. Asha's parents had already arranged a marriage for her, to a wealthy businessman who had promised to provide her with a lavish lifestyle. Asha was torn between following her heart and obeying her parents' wishes.

One day, as Asha and Rohit were walking along the beach, Rohit took her hand and said, "Asha, I love you more than anything in this world. Will you marry me?"

Asha's heart leapt with joy at the thought of spending the rest of her life with Rohit. But then she remembered her parents' expectations, and her face fell.

"I want to be with you more than anything," Asha said, tears streaming down her face. "But my parents have already arranged a marriage for me. I don't know what to do."

Rohit took both of her hands in his and looked deeply into her eyes. "We can't let anyone else decide our fate, Asha. We have to follow our hearts, no matter what the consequences may be."

Asha thought about Rohit's words for a long moment. She knew that he was right. She couldn't let anyone else dictate her life for her.

With newfound courage, Asha went to her parents and told them about her love for Rohit. At first, they were furious. They couldn't believe that their daughter would reject the marriage they had worked so hard to arrange. But eventually, they saw how much Asha loved Rohit, and they reluctantly agreed to let them marry.

The wedding was a grand affair, held in a beautiful outdoor setting overlooking the ocean. Asha wore a traditional red lehenga and gold jewelry, while Rohit donned a white sherwani and a turban. The couple exchanged vows in front of their family and friends, with

Asha's parents finally accepting Rohit as their son-in-law.

As they walked hand in hand, Rohit whispered in Asha's ear, "I promise to love you forever, Asha. No matter what happens, I will always be by your side."

Years passed, and Asha and Rohit's love only grew stronger. They faced many challenges together, but they never once regretted their decision to follow their hearts. They built a beautiful life together, with a loving family and successful careers. And through it all, they never forgot the passion and joy they had felt on that first day, when they had met and fallen in love.

As Asha looked back on her life, she knew that she had found the kind of love she had always dreamed of. A love that was pure and true, and would last a lifetime.

VI

Painting Love

Once upon a time, in a small village in India, there lived a beautiful young woman named Radha. She had long, silky black hair, sparkling brown eyes, and a smile that could light up the whole room. Radha was kind, intelligent, and loved by everyone in the village.

One day, a handsome young man named Raj entered the village. He was tall, dark, and had piercing blue eyes that seemed to stare right into your soul. Raj was a wandering artist who traveled from village to village, painting beautiful pictures and writing poems about the people he met on his travels.

Radha and Raj met by chance in the village market. Raj was immediately struck by Radha's beauty and kindness. They spent the whole day talking and laughing, and before they knew it, it was dark outside.

As they walked home, Raj took Radha's hand and looked into her eyes. "Radha," he said, "I know we've just met, but I feel like I've known you my whole life. Will you give me a chance to get to know you better?"

Radha felt her heart skip a beat. She had never felt this way before, but there was something about Raj that made her feel safe and loved. She nodded her head, and Raj took her hand and kissed it gently.

Over the next few weeks, Radha and Raj spent every moment they could together. They explored the village, went on long walks in the fields, and talked for hours about their dreams and aspirations. Radha had never felt so happy, and she knew that she was falling in love with Raj.

One day, as they were walking in the fields, Raj stopped and turned to Radha. "Radha," he said, "I have something to ask you."

Radha looked at him, her heart beating faster. "What is it, Raj?" she asked.

"I know we've only known each other for a short time," Raj said, "but I can't imagine my life without you. Will you marry me, Radha?"

Radha's eyes filled with tears of happiness. "Yes, Raj," she said, throwing her arms around him. "I will marry you."

Raj and Radha's wedding was the most beautiful ceremony the village had ever seen. The whole village came to celebrate their love, and Raj painted a picture of Radha that captured her beauty and spirit perfectly.

As they exchanged their vows, Raj looked deep into Radha's eyes. "Radha," he said, "I promise to love you and cherish you for the rest of my life. I promise to be there for you in good times and in bad, and to support you in everything you do. I love you more than words can say."

Radha's eyes sparkled with tears of joy. "I love you too, Raj," she said. "You are my soulmate, and I will always be by your side."

As the sun set on their wedding day, Raj and Radha walked hand in hand into their new life together. They knew that they would face challenges along the way, but they also knew that their love was strong enough to overcome anything.

And so they lived happily ever after, painting and writing poetry together, exploring new places, and growing old together. Their love was a shining example of what true love should be: unconditional, supportive, and everlasting.

VII

Love Beyond Borders

Once upon a time in India, there lived a beautiful princess named Sita. She was the daughter of a powerful king and had everything she could ever want, except for true love. Despite having many suitors, Sita could not find a man who truly loved her for who she was.

One day, while strolling through the gardens of her palace, Sita saw a handsome young man who had come to visit the kingdom. His name was Ravi and he was a brave warrior from a neighboring kingdom. Sita was immediately smitten with Ravi and she knew that he was the man she had been searching for.

Over the next few weeks, Sita and Ravi spent a lot of time together and fell deeply in love. They promised each other that they would never be separated and that they would be together forever.

However, their happiness was short-lived. Sita's father did not approve of her relationship with Ravi because he was from a different kingdom and was not of royal blood. He forbade Sita from seeing Ravi and ordered his soldiers to keep him away from the palace.

Despite the king's orders, Sita and Ravi continued to meet in secret, but their love was discovered by the king's spies. The king was furious and ordered Ravi to be captured and executed for disobeying his orders.

Sita was devastated when she heard the news of Ravi's capture and begged her father to spare his life. But the king was not swayed by her pleas and ordered the execution to proceed.

On the day of the execution, Sita snuck out of the palace to be with Ravi one last time. They professed their love for each other and shared a passionate kiss before Ravi was taken away to be executed.

Sita was heartbroken when she saw Ravi's lifeless body hanging from a tree. She cried and cried, unable to believe that her true love was gone forever. She could not bear the pain of living without him and decided to end her own life.

Sita's tragic death shook the kingdom to its core. The king realized too late the mistake he had made in not recognizing true love and the pain it can cause. He ordered a grand funeral for Sita and Ravi, and their love story became the stuff of legends in the kingdom.

The people of the kingdom mourned the loss of Sita and Ravi and vowed to never let true love go unrecognized again. They built a memorial for the couple in the palace gardens and every year, on the anniversary of their deaths, people from all over the kingdom would come to pay their respects and remember the tragic love story of Sita and Ravi.

VIII

Love Conquered and Lost

Once upon a time, in a small village in India, there lived a beautiful young woman named Rhea. She was kind, caring, and had a heart of gold. Rhea had always been fascinated by the stories of love and romance that she had heard from her grandmother, who would often tell her tales of star-crossed lovers and their tragic endings. Little did Rhea know that she was about to experience a love story of her own, one that would leave her heartbroken.

One day, Rhea met a young man named Rohit. He was handsome, with deep brown eyes and a charming smile that made Rhea's heart skip a beat. They started talking and soon became close friends. Over time, their friendship blossomed into love, and they knew that they were meant to be together.

However, fate had other plans for the young couple. Rohit's family was from a higher caste, and they did not approve of him marrying someone from a lower caste.

Despite their objections, Rohit and Rhea decided to elope and start a new life together.

For a while, everything was perfect. They were deeply in love and happy. But their happiness was short-lived. One day, Rohit's family found out about their marriage and was furious. They disowned him, and Rohit was left with no choice but to go back to his family and ask for their forgiveness.

Days turned into weeks, and Rhea waited for Rohit to return. But he never came. She tried to reach him, but his family refused to let her see him. They told her that he was getting married to someone from their caste and that she should forget about him.

Rhea was heartbroken. She had given up everything for the man she loved, and now she was left with nothing. She was consumed by sadness and grief, and her health started deteriorating. She became weak and frail, and everyone in the village was worried about her.

One day, Rhea decided that she could not go on like this anymore. She went to the river, where she had often gone to find solace, and decided to end her life. As she stood by the river, ready to jump in, she saw a reflection of herself in the water. She saw a beautiful young woman, full of life and love, who had been destroyed by circumstances beyond her control.

Suddenly, she heard a voice calling out to her. It was Rohit. He had come to see her, to beg for her forgiveness and to tell her that he still loved her. But it was too late. Rhea was already consumed by the pain and sadness of losing him. She stepped into the river, and as she did, Rohit reached out to grab her, but he was too late. Rhea was swept away by the current.

Rohit was devastated. He had lost the love of his life, and he knew that he would never be able to forget her. He spent the rest of his life trying to make amends for his mistakes, but he knew that he could never make up for what he had done.

And so, the tragic love story of Rhea and Rohit came to an end. They had found love in a world that was not ready for it, and in the end, they were torn apart by circumstances beyond their control. Their love story was a reminder that sometimes, even the strongest love cannot overcome the forces of society and tradition.

IX

Journey to Love

Once upon a time in a small Indian village, there lived a young woman named Meera. She was known for her beauty and intelligence but was also known for her rebellious nature. Meera refused to conform to the traditional Indian customs and instead followed her own heart.

One day, Meera met a handsome man named Raj who had just moved to the village. Raj was also known for his intelligence and charm, but he was also known for his strict adherence to traditional Indian customs. Despite their differences, Meera and Raj quickly fell in love and began to see each other in secret.

As their love grew stronger, Meera and Raj faced many challenges. Meera's family disapproved of their relationship, and Raj's family had arranged for him to marry a woman of their choosing. Despite these obstacles, Meera and Raj refused to give up on their love and continued to see each other in secret.

One day, Meera and Raj decided to run away together and start a new life. They packed their bags and set off on a journey across the countryside, hoping to find a place where they could be together without fear of judgment or persecution.

As they traveled, Meera and Raj encountered many obstacles. They were chased by angry mobs, had to cross treacherous rivers, and even had to fight off wild animals. But through it all, their love for each other never wavered.

Finally, after months of traveling, Meera and Raj arrived at a beautiful and remote village nestled in the foothills of the Himalayas. The villagers welcomed them with open arms, and Meera and Raj knew they had found their new home.

Over the years, Meera and Raj built a life together in the village. They started a family, and their love for each other only grew stronger with each passing day. Despite the challenges they faced, they never forgot the journey that had brought them together and the love that had sustained them through it all.

As they grew old together, Meera and Raj became legends in the village. The people would tell stories of their journey and the love that had triumphed over all obstacles. And even after they passed away, their love continued to inspire generations to come.

In the end, Meera and Raj proved that true love knows no bounds, and that even in the face of great adversity, it can conquer all. Their story will be told for generations to come, a testament to the power of love and the enduring strength of the human spirit.

X

Love Beyond Death

Once upon a time, in a small village in India, there lived a beautiful girl named Laila. She was the daughter of a wealthy merchant and was known for her kind heart and gentle nature. Laila had many suitors, but she had her eyes set on one man, Yusuf. Yusuf was a young man from a neighboring village, and Laila had fallen in love with him the moment she saw him. Despite her father's objections, Laila continued to meet Yusuf secretly.

One day, Laila's father discovered her meetings with Yusuf, and he was furious. He forbade Laila from seeing Yusuf and arranged her marriage to a wealthy man from a neighboring village. Laila was heartbroken, but she knew she had no choice but to accept her fate.

On the day of her wedding, Laila was dressed in a beautiful red lehenga, her hair adorned with flowers. She looked like a princess, but her heart was heavy with sorrow. As she made her way to the wedding venue, she saw Yusuf standing in a corner. He had come to bid her farewell. Laila's heart skipped a beat when she saw him, and she ran to him, tears streaming down her face.

Yusuf held Laila tightly in his arms, and they kissed passionately. It was a moment of pure bliss, but it was short-lived. Laila's father had seen them together and was enraged. He pulled Laila away from Yusuf and ordered his men to kill him.

Laila watched in horror as Yusuf was beaten and stabbed to death. She screamed in anguish, and her father turned to her, his eyes filled with hatred. "You brought this upon yourself," he said, and he walked away, leaving Laila alone with Yusuf's lifeless body.

Laila was inconsolable. She refused to eat or drink and spent her days mourning Yusuf. She would often visit his grave, where she would sit for hours, talking to him as if he were still alive.

One day, while sitting by Yusuf's grave, Laila saw a group of men approaching her. They were the same men who had killed Yusuf. Laila was terrified, but she stood her ground, determined to defend Yusuf's honor.

The men laughed at her and taunted her, and Laila could take it no longer. She grabbed a sword from one of the men and attacked them. She fought with all her might, but she was outnumbered, and soon she was lying on the ground, bleeding and bruised.

Laila's father had been watching the whole scene from afar, and he was filled with remorse. He ran to Laila, but it was too late. She had breathed her last breath, her body lying next to Yusuf's.

Laila's father wept bitterly, realizing his mistake. He had loved his daughter, but his pride had blinded him. He had not seen the depth of her love for Yusuf, and now he had lost both of them.

The villagers mourned the loss of Laila and Yusuf, and their tragic love story became the stuff of legends. It was said that their love was so strong that not even death could separate them.

And so, Laila and Yusuf were buried side by side, their graves adorned with flowers and candles. Their love story had a tragic ending, but it was a love that would be remembered for generations to come.

XI

Love Beyond Boundaries

Once upon a time in a small village in India, there lived a young woman named Anjali. She was beautiful and kind, but her parents had arranged her marriage with a wealthy man who she did not love. Anjali felt trapped and unhappy, but she knew she had to obey her parents' wishes.

One day, while walking in the fields, she met a young man named Rohit. He was handsome and charming, and they immediately fell in love. They started meeting secretly in the fields, under the shade of a large tree, and promised to spend their lives together.

However, their secret love was soon discovered by Anjali's parents. They forbade her from seeing Rohit and arranged for her wedding to take place in two weeks' time. Anjali was heartbroken and didn't know what to do.

Rohit, who loved Anjali deeply, decided to take matters into his own hands. He went to Anjali's house and spoke to her parents, asking them to reconsider their decision.

However, they were adamant that the wedding would take place as planned.

Determined to be with Anjali, Rohit came up with a plan. He decided to elope with her on the night before her wedding. He knew it was risky, but he couldn't bear the thought of losing Anjali.

On the night of the wedding, Rohit arrived outside Anjali's house with a horse and cart. Anjali, who had been waiting anxiously, snuck out of the house and joined him. They rode away into the night, leaving behind everything they had ever known.

For days, they traveled through forests and fields, unsure of where they were going but happy to be together. They eventually arrived in a small town, where they decided to settle down and start a new life together.

Rohit found work as a farmer, and Anjali became a teacher at the local school. They were poor but happy, and their love for each other only grew stronger with each passing day.

One day, Rohit decided to take Anjali on a surprise picnic to the nearby lake. He had brought along a small boat and rowed her out onto the water. As they floated there, surrounded by the beauty of nature, Rohit took out a small box from his pocket.

"Anjali, I know we don't have much, but I want to spend the rest of my life with you," he said, opening the box to reveal a simple gold ring. "Will you marry me?"

Anjali was overjoyed and said yes immediately. They exchanged rings and kissed under the setting sun, feeling grateful for the love they had found.

Years passed, and they grew old together, never forgetting the love that had brought them together. They often spoke of their adventures and the risks they had taken, and they knew that they would do it all over again if it meant being together.

In the end, their love story became legendary in the small town where they lived, and their names were spoken with reverence and admiration by all who knew them. They had proved that true love knows no bounds and that sometimes, the greatest risks lead to the greatest rewards.

XII

Tragic Love

Once upon a time in India, there was a prince named Amar. He was the youngest son of the king and was loved by all. Amar was known for his kindness, intelligence, and bravery.

One day, Amar was out hunting in the forest when he saw a beautiful girl bathing in a nearby river. Her name was Sita, and she was the daughter of a poor farmer. Amar was smitten with her beauty and immediately fell in love.

Amar went to Sita's village to ask for her hand in marriage. However, Sita's father refused as he wanted his daughter to marry someone from their own social class. Amar was heartbroken but did not give up on his love.

He visited Sita secretly and they would spend time together, sharing stories and laughing. They were happy in their own world, but they knew that they could never be together officially.

One day, Amar's father fell ill, and the kingdom was in chaos. Amar's older brothers fought for the throne, and a war broke out. Amar knew that he had to protect his family and his kingdom. He promised Sita that he would come back to her soon.

Amar fought bravely in the war and emerged as the victor. He became the new king, and his kingdom flourished. However, Amar could not forget Sita and missed her terribly.

One day, Amar received a message from Sita, saying that she was getting married to someone else. Amar was devastated and went to Sita's village to stop the wedding. However, Sita's father and her fiance's family refused to listen to him and chased him away.

Amar returned to his kingdom, heartbroken. He could not sleep or eat and spent his days in grief. His ministers and advisors tried to console him, but nothing could ease his pain.

Months passed, and Amar's health started to deteriorate. He had lost the will to live and only thought about Sita. He decided to visit her one last time and went to her village.

When Amar reached Sita's house, he saw that the wedding preparations were still going on. He went to the backyard, where Sita was sitting, and they talked for hours. They both knew that they loved each other, but fate had not been kind to them.

As the sun started to set, Amar knew that he had to leave. He hugged Sita and whispered in her ear, "I will always love you." Sita started to cry, and they both knew that this was the last time they would see each other.

Amar left the village and started to walk back to his kingdom. However, as he was crossing a river, he slipped and fell. He hit his head on a rock and died instantly.

Sita heard about Amar's death and was heartbroken. She could not bear the thought of living without him and decided to end her life. She went to the same river where Amar had seen her for the first time and jumped into it.

The news of their tragic love story spread throughout the kingdom, and the people mourned their deaths. Amar and Sita were remembered as two souls who loved each other but were not destined to be together.

In the end, their love story became a legend, and people would tell their tale for generations to come. Their love had transcended social barriers and had touched the hearts of everyone who heard it.

XIII

Love Beyond Borders

Once upon a time, in a land far away, there were two neighboring countries - India and Pakistan. For decades, these two countries had been at odds with each other, with tensions rising and falling like the tides of the ocean. But amidst all the chaos and conflict, a love story blossomed.

It all started when Ayesha, a Pakistani woman, traveled to India to visit her family. While there, she met Rohit, an Indian man who was studying at the same university as her cousin. From the moment they met, there was a spark between them, a connection that neither of them could ignore.

They spent their days exploring the vibrant streets of Delhi, taking in the sights and sounds of the city. They talked for hours, about everything from their favorite books to their hopes and dreams for the future. And as the days turned into weeks, their love for each other grew stronger and deeper.

But their happiness was short-lived. As news of their relationship spread, their families and friends became concerned. How could they be together, when their countries were at war? They were warned that their love would only bring trouble and heartache.

Despite the warnings, Ayesha and Rohit refused to give up on each other. They believed that their love was stronger than any political or religious divide. They continued to see each other in secret, stealing moments of joy whenever they could.

But one fateful day, their love was discovered. Ayesha's family was outraged, and Rohit's family was equally upset. They were forced to make a decision - stay together and face the wrath of their families and society, or give up on each other and live separate lives.

Ayesha and Rohit chose to stay together. They knew that their love was worth fighting for, no matter the cost. But the road ahead was not easy. They faced discrimination, harassment, and threats of violence. They were ostracized by their families and communities, and forced to flee their homes.

But through it all, they held on to each other. They found strength in their love, and in the knowledge that they were not alone. There were others like them, who had chosen love over hate, and who were fighting for a better future.

Years went by, and the world around them changed. The war between India and Pakistan ended, and the two countries slowly began to rebuild their relationship. Ayesha and Rohit were finally able to come out of hiding, and they were welcomed with open arms.

Their love story had become a symbol of hope and resilience, a testament to the power of love to conquer hate. And as they stood together, hand in hand, watching the sunset over the border between their countries, they knew that their love had been worth all the tears, all the pain, and all the sacrifice.

In that moment, they realized that their love had transcended borders, religion, and politics. It had become something bigger, something more profound - a force for good in a world that so often seemed to be consumed by hate.

And as they looked into each other's eyes, they knew that they would always be together, no matter what. For their love had proven to be stronger than anything else in the world, and it would endure for all eternity.

XIV

From Tinder to Forever

Once upon a time, in the bustling city of New York, there lived a beautiful young woman named Sarah. She was a successful writer with a bright future ahead of her. However, despite her career success, she felt like something was missing from her life. She yearned for a romantic connection with someone who could make her heart sing.

One day, she decided to take the plunge and downloaded Tinder. She swiped left and right, and after a few false starts, she matched with a handsome Indian man named Raj. He was an engineer who had moved to New York City from Mumbai a few years ago. They started chatting and soon realized that they had a lot in common. They both loved traveling, reading, and trying new foods.

Their conversations started to become more and more frequent, and they soon found themselves texting each other all day long. Sarah loved the way Raj made her laugh and how he always seemed to know the right thing to say.

Raj, on the other hand, was smitten with Sarah's intelligence and sense of humor.

After a few weeks of chatting, they decided to meet in person. They arranged to meet at a cozy café in downtown Manhattan. Sarah was a bundle of nerves as she waited for Raj to arrive. When he walked in, she was struck by how handsome he was. He smiled at her and greeted her with a warm hug, and they settled down at a table.

They talked for hours, their conversation flowing effortlessly. They shared stories about their childhoods, their dreams, and their aspirations. They laughed and joked, and Sarah felt her heart swell with happiness. She knew that she had found someone special.

Over the next few weeks, they went on dates all over the city. They visited museums, saw Broadway shows, and ate at fancy restaurants. Sarah loved learning about Raj's Indian culture, and Raj was fascinated by Sarah's American way of life.

As their relationship deepened, they faced challenges too. Sarah's family was initially skeptical of her dating someone from a different culture, and Raj's family had reservations about him dating an American woman. However, they both knew that their love was worth fighting for.

They took things slowly and gave each other time to adjust to their differences. They learned to embrace each other's culture and traditions, and soon, their families came around too.

One evening, while they were walking along the Hudson River, Raj stopped and took Sarah's hand. He looked into her eyes and said, "Sarah, I know we come from different worlds, but I love you more than anything. Will you be mine forever?" Sarah's heart skipped a beat, and she knew that she had found her soulmate. She looked into Raj's eyes and replied, "Yes, Raj. I will be yours forever."

They hugged each other tightly, and as they looked out at the Manhattan skyline, they knew that their love story was just beginning.

In the months that followed, they planned a beautiful wedding that blended their cultures together. They invited their families and friends from all over the world, and it was a celebration of love that neither of them would ever forget.

Years later, as they looked back on their journey together, they knew that they had faced many challenges, but their love had never faltered. They were grateful for Tinder for bringing them together, and they knew that fate had played a hand in their meeting.

As they cuddled together in their cozy New York apartment, Sarah looked up at Raj and whispered, "I love you more than anything in this world." Raj kissed her forehead and replied, "And I love you more than anything in this universe." They held each other tightly and knew that they had found their happily ever after.

XV

Crossing Boundaries

Once upon a time, in the bustling city of Mumbai, lived a young and ambitious woman named Ria. Ria was a successful businesswoman, who owned a chain of restaurants in the city. She was independent, confident, and loved her life to the fullest. One day, while attending a business conference, Ria met a charming British man named Tom.

Tom was in India on a business trip and was immediately drawn towards Ria's beauty and intelligence. They soon started talking, and before they knew it, hours had passed by. Tom was fascinated by India's culture and tradition, and Ria was equally intrigued by Tom's British heritage. They exchanged numbers and promised to stay in touch.

Over the next few weeks, Tom and Ria kept in touch and learned more about each other's lives. They talked about everything from their work to their hobbies, and soon they found themselves falling in love. Ria was hesitant at first, knowing the cultural differences between them, but she couldn't help but be drawn towards Tom's charm and wit.

Tom, on the other hand, was determined to make their love work, no matter what. He decided to move to Mumbai and start a new life with Ria. They faced many challenges along the way, including disapproval from their families and friends, but they remained committed to each other.

They traveled together, exploring India's rich culture and history, and Tom was able to experience first-hand the warmth and hospitality of Ria's family and friends. They also traveled to England, where Tom introduced Ria to his family and friends. They welcomed her with open arms and were impressed by her intelligence and grace.

After several years of dating, Tom proposed to Ria, and she said yes. They had a traditional Indian wedding, complete with vibrant colors, delicious food, and lots of dancing. Their families came together to celebrate their love, and it was a beautiful union of two cultures.

Today, Tom and Ria are happily married, running their businesses together, and raising a beautiful family. They are a true testament to the fact that love knows no boundaries and that cultural differences can only enrich our lives.

XVI

Across Borders

Once upon a time, in a small village near the Indian-Nepali border, there lived a young Indian man named Rohit. Rohit was a handsome and hardworking farmer who spent most of his days tending to his family's fields. One day, while he was walking through the fields, he saw a beautiful Nepali woman named Sita. She was also working in her family's fields nearby. Rohit was mesmerized by her beauty, and he couldn't help but feel drawn towards her.

Sita, on the other hand, noticed Rohit's constant gaze towards her, but she paid no heed to it. She had other things on her mind, like taking care of her family and helping her father with his carpentry work. However, as days passed, Rohit and Sita started bumping into each other more often. They would exchange shy smiles and small talk, but there was an unspoken attraction between them.

As time passed, Rohit and Sita started spending more time together. They would often help each other with their work and have long conversations about their lives and dreams. They discovered that they had a lot in common, despite coming from different countries and cultures. They both shared a love for nature, music, and a desire to travel and see the world.

Slowly but surely, Rohit and Sita's friendship blossomed into a beautiful love story. They would steal moments together whenever they could, sneaking out to sit by the riverbank or under the shade of a tree. They would talk about their future together, and how they would overcome the challenges of being from different countries and cultures.

One day, Rohit mustered the courage to tell Sita about his feelings for her. He confessed that he had fallen deeply in love with her and that he couldn't imagine his life without her. Sita was taken aback by his declaration of love, but she realized that she too had fallen in love with Rohit. They hugged each other tightly, knowing that they had found something special.

Despite facing many challenges and obstacles, Rohit and Sita remained committed to each other. They knew that their love was strong enough to overcome any hurdle that came their way. They worked hard to bridge the cultural gap between them and respect each other's traditions and beliefs.

Years passed, and Rohit and Sita got married in a beautiful ceremony that brought together their families and friends from both India and Nepal. They continued to live and work together in the village, raising their children with love and care. Their love story became a legend in the village, inspiring other young couples to follow their hearts and break down cultural barriers.

And so, Rohit and Sita's love story proved that love knows no borders or boundaries, and that it can bring together people from different countries and cultures in a beautiful and meaningful way.

XVII

Love Blooms Next Door

Once upon a time, there lived a beautiful girl named Radha in a small town in India. Radha was a cheerful and outgoing girl, but she had a secret crush on her next door neighbor, Rohit. Rohit was a handsome and kind-hearted young man who had just moved into the neighborhood a few months ago.

Radha and Rohit would often bump into each other while going to the market or taking a walk in the park. They would exchange pleasantries and chat for a few minutes, but neither of them had the courage to confess their feelings to each other.

One day, while Radha was watering the plants in her garden, she saw Rohit walking towards her house. She felt her heart racing as he approached her. "Hi Radha," Rohit said with a smile. "Your flowers look beautiful. Can I help you with anything?"

Radha blushed at his words and felt a surge of happiness. They spent the next few hours chatting and laughing, and before they knew it, the sun had set and it was time for Rohit to go back to his house.

As days went by, Radha and Rohit spent more time together. They would watch movies, cook together, and go for long walks. Radha loved spending time with Rohit, and she knew that he felt the same way.

One evening, while they were sitting on the rooftop watching the stars, Rohit finally mustered the courage to confess his feelings to Radha. "Radha, I've been wanting to tell you something for a long time," Rohit said softly. "I think I'm in love with you."

Radha's heart skipped a beat as she heard his words. "I feel the same way, Rohit," she said with a smile. "I've been in love with you since the day you moved into the neighborhood."

Rohit took Radha's hand in his, and they looked into each other's eyes, lost in the moment. From that day on, they were inseparable. They knew that they had found true love in each other, and they promised to cherish each other forever.

And so, Radha and Rohit's love story began, a beautiful tale of two people who found their soulmate in their next door neighbor.

Printed by Libri Plureos GmbH in Hamburg,
Germany

9 798889 868774